# Sports Day

Today is school sports day.

Peppa and her friends are all here.

The first event is running.

The children have to run as fast as they can.

"Ready . . . Steady . . . Go!"
says Madame Gazelle.

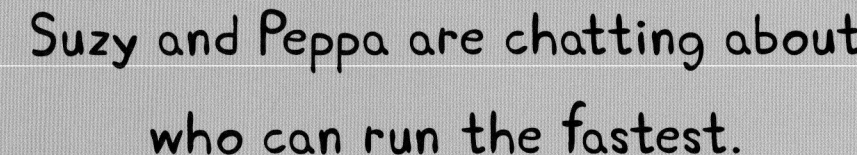

Suzy and Peppa are chatting about who can run the fastest.

Rebecca Rabbit is in the lead.

Peppa and Suzy are right at the back.

Rebecca Rabbit wins the race!

"Hooray," everyone cheers.

Peppa and Suzy are last.

"It's not the winning that matters,"
Daddy Pig reminds them.
"But the taking part."

"The next event is the long jump,"
says Madame Gazelle.

George and Richard Rabbit have to run
and then jump as far as they can.
Whoever jumps the furthest is the winner.
"Ready . . . Steady . . . Go!"

Oh dear. Richard Rabbit has jumped further than George. "Hooray!" shout all his friends.

George is not happy.

"Remember George," says Peppa. "It's not the winning that matters but the taking part."

The next race is the relay.
Daddy Pig is in the lead. He hands
the baton to Peppa.

"Thank you Daddy, you did very well.
Now it's my turn to. . . " begins Peppa.
"Stop talking and run!" snorts Daddy Pig.

Emily Elephant is the winner!
Everyone cheers. "Hooray!"

Peppa comes last.
She is not feeling happy.

It's the last event of the day, the tug of war.

Boys against girls.

"The girls will win!" snorts Peppa.

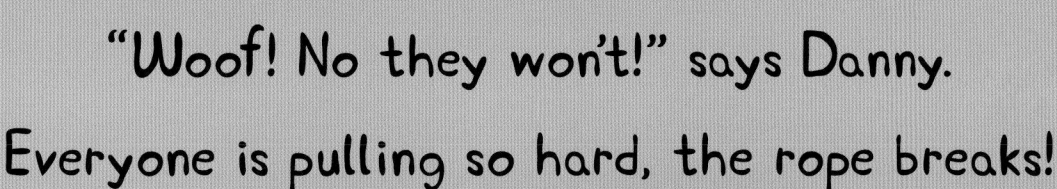

"Woof! No they won't!" says Danny.
Everyone is pulling so hard, the rope breaks!

"The result is a draw!
Both teams win!" says Madame Gazelle.
Everybody cheers.

"Hooray!"

"I love school sports day," snorts Peppa,

"Especially when I win a prize!"